ANIMAL BABIES

By Rebecca Dickinson
Illustrated by Lisa Bonforte

A GOLDEN BOOK · NEW YORK
Western Publishing Company, Inc., Racine, Wisconsin 53404

 Library of Congress Catalog Card Number: 87-81765 ISBN: 0-307-12116-X
E F G H I J K L M

foal

Animal babies are big or small,
Fuzzy or smooth, short or tall.

lamb
chick

They come in many shapes and sizes—
And sometimes bring us big surprises!

puppies

foal

This baby horse is full of fun.
It likes to jump and play and run.

Some baby lambs are soft and white,
While other lambs are black as night.

ducklings

Baby ducks can swim just fine.
They follow Mother in a line.

These piglets like to run and squeal,
While Mama quietly eats her meal.

piglets

fox pups

Baby foxes tease each other—
And then get scolded by their mother.

bear cubs

Bear cubs love to romp and play,
While turtles like to sleep all day.

rabbits

These rabbits hop to find their lunch.
Their noses wiggle as they munch!

These fuzzy chicks cry cheep,
cheep, cheep.
They'd rather play than go to sleep.

chicks

Some babies like to curl up snug—
These kittens have their friends to hug.